HOLIDAY HEART WISHES

A DICKENS HOLIDAY NOVELLA

LUCINDA RACE

MC TWO PRESS

Holiday Heart Wishes is for my daughters, Megan and Emily, who always find a way to be home for the holidays making my heart wish come true.

1

*V*isibility was down to zero. What made Vera think driving home tonight was the best idea? She hunched closer to the steering wheel, trying to peer through the blanket of snow. A better plan would have been to wait until morning, when at least she could see. But when the going gets tough, the only place she wanted to go was home. With her bags packed in the trunk and her sweet rescue pup, Mollie, riding shotgun, she should be home in less than a half hour.

Up ahead, there was a dark mound on the shoulder of the road. *Oh shoot.* It was a truck and the hood was up. She slowed, not that she was going fast; it was more like a gentle glide to a stop. She pressed the passenger window button and it slid down. Snow fell inside and Mollie blinked at her.

"Hey, are you okay?"

A dark-haired hunk appeared from under the hood. He held up his hand in greeting.

His smile was slow and easy, which gave her heart an unexpected flutter.

"Thanks for stopping. I figured I'd be out here all night and turn into a popsicle."

Mollie's tail began to thump against the seat. She was never this excited with strangers. This guy was definitely someone she would like to have met back in the city.

He leaned into the window. "I'm Tony Barbee."

She gave a little wave. "Nice to meet you. I'm Vera."

"Any chance you can give me a lift into Dickens? I think my alternator is dead. I've got no power."

She looked into the blinding snow ahead of her. She couldn't just agree to pluck a stranger from the side of the road on a dark and wintry night.

"Hey, I get it. Strange guy. Not the best of ideas." He took a step back. "Any chance you could call a tow truck? My cell died too."

"Sounds like you're having a tough day." She gave him a tentative smile; she knew how that felt. "I'll do one better. What if I park behind you and wait while the truck comes? This way, you won't get hit from behind. Take it from me, your truck is virtually invisible until you're right on top of it."

He gave her a snow-melting smile. "That sounds great. Thanks." He pointed to his truck. "I'm gonna wait in there. No sense getting even more covered with snow."

She called the Dickens Police Department and the dispatcher said someone would be out soon. After backing her car up, Vera waited in its warmth, flashers on. Mollie, her goofy retriever mix, looked at her from her comfy plush bed in the passenger seat as if to say they were warm but what about the other guy?

"I'm not going out there. You watch the news with me. It's full of crazy people." She shook her head. Here she was having a conversation with her dog about a man who might be freezing in his truck. "We'll give it ten minutes and if no one shows up to help, like the tow truck, I'll invite him to get into the backseat." She glanced at Mollie. "Acceptable?"

The pup lay her head down on her paws and closed her eyes.

"Easy for you to snooze. It's a good thing Mom doesn't know I'm coming tonight. Otherwise she'd be waiting up and fretting about me driving in this weather."

Vera adjusted the fan on the heater. It was cold out but inside her car, she was toasty warm. She did feel guilty about poor Tony sitting in a cold vehicle. She played a game on her phone and took note of the clock. It had been six minutes. Another couple and she'd offer to let Tony sit in her car. He looked like a trustworthy kind of guy.

She played a word game this time. It took longer than solitaire. Just as she typed in the last few letters, blue lights strobed through the white flakes. They looked almost like blue flake ornaments on a Christmas tree.

She eased down the window and was happy to see a familiar face, her mom's neighbor.

"Hello, Tom. Good to see you're still keeping the roads of Dickens safe."

"Vera." His eyes grew bright. "Your mother didn't tell me you were coming in tonight."

"It's a surprise."

"Any chance you'll stay a little longer this trip? It's been a long time since you've been home for more than a couple of days during the holiday." He adjusted his blue knit cap under his cop hat.

"I'm not sure." She pointed to Tony, who stomped through the deepening snow.

Tom stuck out his hand. "Well, if it isn't old home week. Tony Barbee, good to see you again. Coming in to spend some time with your uncle?"

"I am. But as you can see, I'm having a little engine trouble and my cell died, so this nice lady took pity on me and called you."

Tom leaned against her car. "Good thing she stopped. Not much traffic out here this time of night, especially in a snowstorm. Bad news: We probably won't get the tow truck out here for a few hours." He glanced at Tony. "I could drop you off, but I have to check out a few more roads before I head in."

"A ride-along sounds exciting." A smile quirked his lips.

"Sorry, for an official ride-along we'd have to fill out a bunch of paperwork ahead of time, but maybe Vera could drop you off in town at your uncle's place."

Stammering, she said, "Tom, I don't know about that."

"Tony's harmless." With a chuckle, he said, "As long as he's not banging on his keys. He's a ruthless newspaper reporter with a keen eye on the truth." He tapped the door. "Besides, I'll check for your car in your mom's driveway and if it's not there, I'll come looking for you."

Inwardly she groaned. Tom was right. Tony seemed harmless and they knew each other. She looked at Mollie snoozing on the passenger seat.

"Come on girl, hop in the back. We've got a passenger."

Tony's face lit up. "Thanks, Vera." He jogged back to his truck and opened the door and withdrew a large duffel bag. Then he dropped the hood of his truck and positioned two flares in the snow that Tom had given him.

Tom said, "I'll have the truck towed to the garage. You can check on it tomorrow."

Tony stuck out his hand and shook Tom's. "Good to see you again."

"I expect we'll be bumping into each other." He gave Vera a smile. "Drive safe."

She popped her trunk so Tony could stow his bag. He slammed it shut. Vera tossed the dog bed in back and he got into the passenger seat. Rubbing his hands together, he grinned. "That heat feels good."

"Sorry if you think I was rude not asking you to wait in the car but," using air quotes, she said, "stranger danger."

"No worries. My mom did the same thing to me. Tom vouched for me, so we're all good."

She clicked off her hazard lights and eased back onto where the road should be if she could have seen it. "It's going to be slow going. I have snow tires, but the way it's coming down, we're just going to take our time."

He pointed over his shoulder. "What's your pup's name?"

"That's my protector, Mollie." She laughed as the dog's gentle snoring filled the car. "She must not view you as a threat since she's sleeping right through this part of our adventure. In her defense, she's getting up there in years and I swear she's got a little cat mixed into her DNA. She can sleep most of the day away. Unless of course there are cookies involved."

The snoring stopped and her head popped up. She sneezed.

Vera and Tony laughed.

"Is that her way of saying *you mentioned one of my favorite things*?"

"How'd you guess?"

"Growing up, my uncle had dogs, and they were trained to sneeze when they were ready for a cookie. At first he thought it was funny until every time someone was near the dog's cookie jar, they'd start sneezing. I'm not sure how he stopped it."

"Your uncle sounds like he loved his pups."

"He did. I don't think he has one now. He recently moved into a new place."

"Speaking of which, what's his address?"

He held up his dead phone. "No idea. If you don't mind, just drop me at the town motel and I'll call him in the morning."

She looked his way. "Nonsense. You can stay on my mom's couch. I'd offer you the guest room, but she recently took in a roommate. She said she was tired of talking to an empty house. I haven't met her yet but I'm sure she's a nice lady."

"That's funny since my uncle just moved too. Looks like there is a lot of real estate transactions happening in Dickens. I don't want to be any trouble, so the motel is just fine."

"Tom said you were a good guy, so unless you have objections to sleeping on a couch, you're welcome to stay until we can get your truck in the morning."

"Thanks. I'll take you up on the offer."

They drove through downtown. The old-fashioned streetlamps were decked out with garlands and white twinkle lights. The gazebo in the village green housed a small Christmas tree and more garland draped around the white wood sides. But it was the enormous tree that was a showstopper. It was a scene right out of a Norman Rockwell painting. Every shop sported decorations.

"It's magical," she breathed and slowed to a stop in front of the large lit Christmas tree. She closed her eyes and wished with all her heart that she'd find a new direction while she was in her hometown. When she opened them, she noticed Tony also had his eyes closed. Was he making a wish too?

His eyelashes fluttered and he gave her a sheepish smile. "Don't laugh, but ever since I was a kid, when I saw this tree, I'd close my eyes and make my Christmas wish."

She placed a hand on her chest. "Me too. But why don't I remember you?"

"I went to private school so I was only here for holiday breaks with my uncle, and in summer I was at camp. Trust me. If we had met before, I would have remembered you, Vera—?"

She stuck out her hand. "Davis. I'm Vera Davis."

A flash of recognition seemed to flit across his face, but he didn't speak. She took her foot off the brake and drove the short distance to her mom's house.

As she parked in the snow-filled driveway, her heart ached just a little. It had been too long since she had been home.

"Ready to go inside?"

He peered through the windshield. "Great house." He pushed open the door and Mollie stretched on the backseat, then proceeded to squeeze between Tony and the dashboard to be the first one out of the car.

She frolicked in the snow, sticking her nose in and tossing little triangles of white stuff off in the air.

Vera pulled her bag from the trunk and waited for Tony to do the same. She remarked, "Someone's happy to be here."

The front porch light flicked on. The snow-covered steps were humps leading to the oversized green door, and a wreath with a burgundy bow filled its width.

"I wonder if Tom called my mother and let her know we were on the way." She trudged through the snow and whistled for Mollie to follow. Tony trailed behind.

The front door opened.

"Mom." Her jaw dropped.

"Uncle Frank?" Tony said.

2

*T*ony was stunned. What was Uncle Frank doing at Vera's mother's house? It was just the first of his questions for his uncle, but that was for when they were alone. He could only imagine what Vera was thinking. If the look on her face was an indication, she too was caught off guard.

Mrs. Davis said, "Come in out of the cold."

She stepped through the door while Uncle Frank took Vera's bags. Mollie bounded up the stairs, completely unconcerned with another strange man in front of her. Maybe all she was looking for was a place to curl up and snooze until breakfast.

Vera's steps slowed as she looked from Frank to her mother. "Thank you." She crossed the threshold and shrugged out of her coat. Mom took it from her.

"Honey, why didn't you tell me you were coming home tonight? It wasn't until I heard your car and looked out the window—well, imagine my surprise. I'm so happy you're home." Her mom looked at the tall, thin, distinguished-looking man beside her. Tony's Uncle Frank, looked to be in his late fifties, had short, styled, salt and pepper hair and deep blue eyes. Even at this late hour, he looked raring to go.

"You're not the only one who got a surprise." She dropped her voice. "Mom, what is this man doing here?"

"Come inside and I'll make some tea to warm us all up." She looked at Tony and gave him a warm smile. "I'm Georgia, Vera's mother. I didn't know she was bringing her boyfriend home."

Vera placed her hand on her mother's arm. "Tony's not my boyfriend, this is Frank's nephew. I found him on the side of the road. What I meant was his truck broke down just outside of town and I told him he could stay here tonight before going to his uncle's place." She gave Frank another once over and continued, "But it seems his uncle is in our front hall."

"Oh, that's what I meant." Mom actually giggled. "Well, I had hoped to introduce you to Frank tomorrow and ease into the conversation but"—she threw up her hands—"it is what it is."

She hurried from the room with another promise of tea.

Mollie had settled into the corner of the couch and Vera looked around for her bag. She followed the footsteps in the hall and saw Frank was carrying her bag upstairs with Tony following him. What the heck was happening here? It was like they were in the Twilight Zone or something.

She huffed a sigh and walked down the center hall into the heart of the house, the kitchen.

"Mom, please tell me what is going on here. Just a few weeks ago, you told me you got a roommate, Fran." And then it dawned on her, Fran was really Frank. "Is that man living with you?"

Her mother's hazel eyes sparkled. It was easy to see her mom was happy, but this was the first Vera was hearing about a man living in their house. What would her dad think if he knew this?

"Yes, Frank and I have been friends for a couple of years and dating for almost a year. We decided to take the plunge and move in together. Since I was more attached to this house, he moved here."

"What would Dad think if he knew you had moved some guy into our home?"

Mom stopped pouring hot water midstream. "If your father could tell me anything, he'd say *be happy*. I'm tired of being the lonely widow. Frank is a good man. We have a lot of fun together and I would appreciate it if you'd keep an open mind, get to know him, and watch us together. You'll see I made the right choice."

She went back to fixing the pot of tea. "Grab the cookie tin. We might as well enjoy something sweet too."

Vera crossed the room and saw that some things hadn't changed. Mom was using the old tin box with the Christmas tree on the front. It was the container she turned to every year when she started baking cookies.

Frank came in just as Mom picked up the tray with the tea pot and mugs. "I'll take that, Georgia."

Tony gave her a half-shoulder shrug as if to say he still didn't know what the heck was going on either.

Mollie strolled in and Mom picked up a dog treat from the counter. "Come on, girl. Let's get comfy and we can all get to know each other."

Vera and Tony didn't have a choice but to follow the older couple into the living room and watch as they sat on the couch, almost touching. Vera sat on the overstuffed plaid chair on one end of the couch and Tony perched on the leather armchair on the opposite side. Mollie curled up next to Mom and, after inhaling her cookie, fell back to sleep again. So much for a dog's sixth sense to the invader in their home.

Vera took the mug from her mom and leaned back in the chair, wrapping her hands around the warmth of the cup and inhaling the calming aroma of peppermint.

Frank took Mom's hand. Vera watched him give it a gentle squeeze.

"Vera, Tony," he began, "Georgia and I have known each other for many years since we both live in town and coincidentally joined the horticultural club about two years ago. We began talking and before we knew it, we started dating. Fast forward—"

Vera silenced a snort.

"—to about three months ago when we realized we spent more time together than apart, and it just seemed to make sense to move in together. It took a while to work out the logistics, but here we are." He was practically beaming.

Tony crossed his outstretched legs. "Then why is this the first I'm hearing you're even dating someone, let alone living with Mrs. Davis?"

Vera bobbed her head in agreement. "Mom, why haven't you said anything to me?"

"You're so busy with work, I didn't think it was that important, and when you said you were coming home for the holidays, I knew it was the perfect time to share our happy news."

Under her breath, she said, "More like springing a trap."

"What was that?" Her mother's sharp gaze was telling. With her bat-like hearing, she had heard exactly what Vera said.

"Nothing. It's been a long day and the drive was exhausting. I think I'm going to turn in."

"Wait. We still don't know the whole story about how you two ended up here." Frank slipped his arm around the back of the couch and rested it on her mother's shoulders.

"Remember," Tony said, "My truck broke down just outside of town. Vera was driving by and was kind enough to stop and call for help. Tom Johnson rolled up and basically assured Vera I was trustworthy, so she offered me a ride to town. I couldn't pull up your new address since my phone died, so she volunteered the couch for the night. In the morning, I was going to track you down."

"That's right too." Frank chuckled. "You should have seen the looks on your faces when Georgia and I came out onto the porch." His chest rose up and down with amusement.

Mom tapped his leg. "Stop teasing the kids. They don't find our new living situation amusing. Just look at how Vera has her right eyebrow cocked." Mom jabbed a finger toward her face and chuckled. "She gets that from her dad."

"Mom, we're all tired. I'll get a sheet, blanket, and pillow to make up the couch for Tony."

"No need. He can take the guest room."

Vera could feel the color drain from her face. She wanted to groan but what good would that do? It would only make this awkward situation even more weird.

"I can show you where towels and such are stored, if you want to follow me."

Tony set his mug on the tray. "Goodnight."

"G'night, Tony. We'll have breakfast at eight if you're up." Frank stood and slapped him on the shoulder, still beaming. He then gave Vera an awkward half hug. "Good night, Vera. I'm sorry this came as a shock, but tomorrow we'll talk more and you'll see for yourself how happy your mother has made me."

"Goodnight, Frank." She kissed Mom's cheek and ascended the stairs.

Tony trailed behind her and she paused midstep to snap her fingers for Mollie to come to bed.

The dog's nails clicked over the polished maple floors and she dashed up the steps and down the hall toward Vera's room.

"The guest room is across from mine." It wasn't a long

hallway and the carpet was thick and plush, so their footsteps were soundless. She stopped at the first door on the left. "This is the bathroom that we'll share, and the next door is the guest room. Towels are in the closet behind the door."

"Thanks Vera. I appreciate, well, everything. It has been a crazy night."

She pointed back at the direction they'd come from. "Mom's room is down there." She frowned. "And your uncle." She pointed to the door on the right. "And this is my room."

He nodded. "Uncle Frank put your bags in there." He stroked the top of Mollie's head. "See you in the morning."

TONY FLICKED the light switch and entered the spacious bedroom. There were two windows that looked out over what he guessed was the backyard, and one side window. The bed looked comfy, with a fluffy down comforter and tons of pillows. Not that he needed luxury to get a good night's sleep. He could sleep in a recliner chair, and often did when he was researching a story for the newspaper. He slipped off his sneakers and grabbed his shaving kit. He'd brush his teeth and hit the sack.

After coming out of the bathroom, he noticed that Vera's door was open halfway. He tapped on it and waited for her to invite him in.

Vera was perched on the end of her bed, petting Mollie. She gave him a half grin. "Do you need something?"

"Can I come in and talk for a minute?"

"Sure. If you want, close the door."

Now that she was on her home turf, she wasn't nearly as cautious. It also helped that her mother and his uncle were just down the hall.

She had changed into gray-checked flannel bottoms and a red thermal long sleeve tee with red fleece socks on her feet.

Her hair fell in blonde sheets around her face, framing her soft brown eyes. "I couldn't help but notice you didn't seem very thrilled that my uncle has moved in with your mom. I'm thinking if we put our heads together, maybe we could show them they're rushing into this arrangement too fast and they should slow down before someone gets hurt."

Her eyes brightened. "Do you think that would work? I mean, it's not like your uncle doesn't seem like a nice man but"—she nodded and her brow wrinkled—"I do think they should take it a little slower. They haven't been dating each other that long and to already be living together." She made a *tsk tsk* sound. "We should join forces and see what we can do."

She stuck out her hand to shake on it. It fit perfectly in his and her skin was soft like fine cotton. A jolt of electricity surged in his veins as she clasped her hand with his. Vera's eyes widened and he knew she felt it too.

She pulled back and tucked the hand under her leg. Her eyelashes fluttered, not like she was flirting with him but with the surprise of their connection. It was like something from one of those romance movies on television. And not something he had ever experienced before.

He glanced at the floor and shuffled his feet. "Okay, then. See you in the morning."

"Breakfast is at eight." She gave him a smile. "Mom's best meal is breakfast, and you don't want to miss it."

"Thanks for the tip." He pulled her door closed and smiled. He could see why Uncle Frank was attracted to Georgia, she looked just like her beautiful daughter.

3

*W*hen Vera woke, the sun was out and the snow sparkled like millions of tiny crystals. She squinted and wished for sunglasses. Now, wouldn't that be a hoot to go to breakfast wearing shades? All she really wanted to do was pull the blankets up over her head and snuggle in, but the smell of bacon and coffee tickled her senses and made her mouth water. Mollie was tucked in close to her body, snoring like a lanky, fur-covered freight train.

"Hey girl, time to get up."

She would swear the dog groaned at her. Vera flicked the covers off and over Mollie and picked up her clothes for the short trip across the hall to the bathroom. The carpet was toasty under her toes. She never bothered with slippers when she was upstairs. Mom strongly believed bedrooms should be carpeted to keep the noise as low as possible, and on cold winter mornings, feet would be warm.

Vera hurried through her morning routine and added an extra dab of makeup. Might as well look her best for getting a close-up on Frank. And, for that matter, Tony. Last night, she had noticed his long and lean frame was filled out in all the right places and his jeans seemed to hug his backside perfectly. And the dark hair and blue eyes were straight from the pages of a magazine. Not that she had looked. Much.

Before she headed down the back stairs, she whistled to Mollie, who finally decided to make an appearance, bounding down the steps ahead of her.

"Morning," she said to no one in particular and opened the back door so Mollie could go out and tend to her business. While she kept one eye on her fur baby, she trained the other on the stove.

"What's for breakfast?"

Tony hadn't put in his appearance yet, but based on the thudding on the front stairs, it would be moments before he joined Mom and Frank.

"Something simple. Blueberry pancakes, bacon, and Frank whipped up some blueberry-infused maple syrup. There's juice in the refrigerator and I picked up light cream for you, too."

"Thanks Mom."

Tony stepped in and gave Vera a smile as he dipped his head. "Good morning Mrs. Davis, Uncle Frank."

Mom waved her hand at him. "Georgia, please. After all, we're almost family."

Mollie decided at that moment to bark. She was ready to come in for her breakfast. Vera fumbled with the doorknob. Tony smoothly put his hand over hers and helped her to pull it.

"Breathe," he said for her ears alone.

She flashed him an appreciative look. This was not going to be easy. First, how to slow down the older generation's romance, and two, fight this urge to flirt with the man currently holding her hand. "Got it."

Mollie forced the door and rushed to see Mom, her second-best friend in the world, who broke off a piece of crisp bacon. Mollie quickly dropped to just about sitting on the floor and actually licked her mouth in anticipation of the treat.

"Here you go, Mollie."

With a very dainty bite, the dog took it from Mom and trotted over to where her water and food dish would be.

She said to Tony, "At least someone here doesn't sense the awkwardness."

To cover their lack of conversation, he asked, "Any coffee?"

"Help yourself, and could you pour a cup for Vera? She seems to be moving in slow motion this morning. Must have been the stress from leaving the city last night."

Mom had no idea. To lose a job the week before Christmas was harsh, but in hindsight, it might not be a bad thing. She could stay here a while longer, maybe even permanently, so Mom wouldn't be lonely and need to have Frank living with her.

Tony passed her the coffee and Mom handed her the cream. Everyone was moving around the spacious and sunny kitchen like they had been doing this for years.

"Sit. Frank will deliver our pancakes hot off the griddle."

The small round table was set for four, and it was cozy quarters. It was obvious to Vera this was just the way Mom and Frank liked it, as they made goo-goo eyes at each other while he put a stack of flapjacks on each plate.

They ate quietly for several minutes; Vera was savoring the blueberry sauce, which she did mention was delicious, and Frank looked pleased.

"Tell me where are you off to this morning." Mom asked, "Maybe a little last minute shopping, stroll around town. I know! You should stop in the adorable tea shop, you know, Miss Amelia Crumpton's Tea Emporium? Edna Withers owns it now. They have some wonderful new blends for the holidays and the most delicious little cakes. You two might really enjoy it."

"Mrs. Withers, my old teacher?"

"One and the same."

Vera opened her mouth to say they weren't going out and about together when Tony piped up.

"That sounds great. I need to stop by the mechanic to see when they can fix my truck, so maybe we can walk around."

"It's not too cold out. You could probably leave Vera's car and just walk. You know, make room for the tea shop and all." Mom had a mischievous gleam in her eye. What was she up to now?

"That, Mrs., I mean Georgia, sounds like a good idea." Tony stabbed a forkful of pancakes. "What do you think, Vera? Will you be up for a stroll around town?"

"Sure. Maybe we'll take Mollie with us. She could use the exercise too."

Frank rested a hand on Mom's arm and grinned. "That means we can wrap presents while they're out."

"Speaking of that, Mom, why don't you have a tree yet?"

"I wanted to wait for you. We always cut one down at Gridley Tree Farm. Maybe even a sleigh ride. That would be something fun to do after lunch. The four of us out tromping through the rolling hills and row after row of evergreen trees, picking out the first of what I hope will be many trees we'll share."

Vera began to choke and Tony thumped her back. Tears sprang to her eyes. Was this a permanent arrangement?

She nodded and croaked, "Sounds like fun."

MOLLIE WAS PULLING on her leash while Tony and Vera wandered down the freshly plowed sidewalk. The breeze was crisp and the sky clear. Little puffs of breath lingered in the air as they exhaled.

"What's your take on all of this between my mother and your uncle?" Vera asked.

"No offense, but they are rushing into this, not looking left or right. Blinders on. I mean, you become friends and then move in together. What happened to his house?"

"You should ask him. Maybe he kept it on the off chance things don't work out." Vera could only hope. It was so weird seeing a man other than her father in her childhood home. She did have to admit, grudgingly, that her mom smiled a lot more than she remembered. But they needed to slow down.

She stepped on a slick patch of concrete and slipped. Tony looped his arm through hers and hauled her back up. "Don't worry. You won't fall."

His eyes were the prettiest shade of blue and they twinkled when he looked at her. Like he had a secret and wasn't willing to share. At least not yet.

"Thanks." Mollie was looking at them as if to say *come on, let's keep going*.

"Why don't you hold onto my arm? If nothing else, you can keep me on my feet."

She smiled at him. "Teamwork. I like it."

"Just like we're putting our heads together about the other issue we have."

Vera took a few more cautious steps. "What are we going to do about that?"

Tony mused, "What if we try and highlight all the things they don't have in common?"

"Frank said how they met in that class about plants, but I'll bet there are a ton of things she likes to do that he would find boring."

"That's right." Tony's voice perked up. "Uncle Frank hates new movies. He only watches stuff from the forties and fifties. He loves the Abbot and Costello and Laurel and Hardy movies. Slapstick comedy at its best."

"Mom's favorites are thrillers and romcoms. But she does love the old holiday musicals."

"Tonight, let's suggest we watch *Holiday Inn*. Uncle Frank will hate it."

"Mom will love it." She tightened her grip on his arm and hugged it to her side. "Great idea. I'll bet it's on Netflix."

"Even better."

She steered them to the right toward South Main Street so they could make their first stop to check on Tony's truck.

"If you don't mind, I would like to swing by that tea store and get a to-go cup. Mom made it sound like it was a must do for this morning."

"I'm not a huge fan of tea, but what we had last night was good." He gave her a grin. "What the heck. We'll get tea and a cookie for the rest of our walk."

Vera drank in the sights of all the holiday decorations. Seeing everything again gave her a fresh wave of nostalgia. Could she see herself settling down here and starting her own social media marketing business? She didn't need to be in an office building to contact clients. That's what Zoom meetings were for, and living here would give her a quality of life she was lacking in the city. It was something to mull over.

"Tell me about your writing. You're a newspaper columnist?"

"I'm a reporter."

"What do you write?"

He was strangely mum on the details.

"You do know this is how conversation works," she teased. "I ask questions, you answer, and then you can ask me questions and I answer."

"I write under a pen name most of the time. Occasionally I get a byline. Under my name, I write about gardening."

Vera stepped over a pile of slush as they crossed the street. The garage was a short way down the road. "Like uncle, like nephew."

"He always had me hanging around him, puttering in his greenhouse." He lit up. "Does your mother have a greenhouse?"

"No." She gave him a sidelong glance. "Why?"

"That is his passion. Working in the greenhouse. I can't see he'll give that up."

"Good to know." They stepped up on the curb and Mollie stopped to sniff the telephone pole.

They started walking and she said, "Here's the garage."

He pointed to a sleek, deep green restored Ford truck. "There's my ride."

"It's old." She could have bit her tongue. "I'm sorry. That was rude."

"You're right." He laughed. "But I rebuilt it myself and just can't part with it. My other ride is a motorcycle. But only in good weather."

"I've never ridden on one."

He disengaged his arm from hers. "Maybe someday I'll take you for a ride."

He pulled open the door and she said, "I'll wait here with Mollie."

"Be right back."

She walked away from the door and Mollie stuck by her side. Tony was a nice guy and she was glad to have a partner in crime with Operation Slow Down.

Within a short while, Tony came outside and looked around. When their eyes met, his smile touched her heart. If nothing else, she had someone she could enjoy time with.

"Another day or two and I can pick up the truck. Until then, I'm on foot."

"Not to worry. If you need a ride, I'll drive you. After all, we're going to be spending a lot of time together until after the holidays."

He grinned. "It could be much worse."

4

*A*fter a quick bite for lunch, Mom and Frank drove his truck to Gridley's Tree Farm while Vera and Tony took her car. Mom thought it was the perfect way to create a memory with her sweetie—her words, not Vera's.

The sun had melted the snow from the blacktop as Vera drove behind Frank. "What do you think of Dickens at Christmastime so far?" She adjusted the fan on the heaters to blow onto their feet. Hers were still chilled from their walk around town earlier.

"It's very quaint here. Almost as if we stepped back in time when life was simple and people actually cared about their neighbors. Most people in my apartment building seem jaded and are cool toward each other." He looked her way. "What about you? Do you like living in the city?"

"I did. But more and more, I'm missing small town life." She tightened her hands on the steering wheel. "I'm thinking of moving back and starting my own company."

"What is it you do?"

"I handle social media for businesses. Create some advertisements, budget, and schedule to run. Then I track trends and the like. It's fun, portable, and never the same."

"Sounds interesting. How did you get into social media?"

"I was in marketing and as the world of online communication exploded using tiny bites of information, I gravitated toward it and worked to become an expert. Most people thought I was nuts to deviate from the traditional marketing, but it has paid off." She stared straight ahead. *Until recently, when her company thought they could hire a high school graduate for a lot less money.*

"I sense there is more to the story," Tony said.

"Oh look. Here we are." Grateful to be at the tree lot where she could escape this line of conversation, she parked next to Frank. "Ready to play Paul Bunyan?"

He snapped his fingers. "Ah, shucks. I didn't bring my hatchet."

"Don't worry. They let you borrow one, and if you have never wielded one"—she jutted her thumb toward her chest —"I've got you covered."

"This, I can't wait to see."

They joined Mom and Frank and after securing a small saw, not a hatchet as Vera promised, they headed in the direction of the blue spruce varieties. Frank casually mentioned in passing that it was one of his favorites and Mom jumped on it even though she wasn't a fan. Mildly surprised, Vera figured it was just the beginning of change for their traditional holiday.

Trudging through half-plowed rows, Mom veered off down one long row that had a sign for the blue spruces. She wanted to remind her mom they preferred Douglas Firs but hey, she'd give in for this one. There were a few traditions she wouldn't part with, though.

Tony caught her eye. "What are you plotting?"

"Nothing. Mom likes a fir tree and I'm kinda surprised she's agreed to the spruce."

"It's called compromise." He glanced at his uncle and her mom. "They look happy. Do we have the right to poke at it?"

"You thought it was a great idea last night and this morning too." She threw a look his way as he tripped over a root. She grabbed his arm and pulled him upright, but he just happened to land with a thump against her body.

"Did you hurt your ankle?"

He waved a hand. "It's no big deal. Nothing I can't walk off. I'm tough."

He took a limping step forward and she bit her lower lip. It had to hurt.

She slipped her arm around his waist. "I'll get you back to the car."

"I'll be fine."

"If you persist on hobbling through the field, then I will insist on holding your hand."

He eyed her suspiciously. "How sweet of you."

With a loud snort, Vera said, "Don't flatter yourself. It'll give you some support. Otherwise I'll end up having to get one of the workers to come get you on an ATV." Her eyes lit up. "Or we could catch a sleigh ride back up the hill once we get the tree. You said it was something you've never done before."

"You talked me into it." He tucked his arm under hers and clasped her hand. "Just go easy."

"If you start to feel a worsening pain, let me know." They took a few slow steps. "Are you anything like Frank?"

"Some people think so. Why?"

"No reason." But if Frank was sweet like Tony, it could explain how her mom had fallen for him. On top of that, for an older man, he was good looking. She cocked her head and caught sight of them up ahead. She watched as they chatted and exchanged a glance or a laugh. They looked good together.

As SELFISH as it might sound, Tony was kind of glad he had twisted his ankle. It was a good excuse to be close to Vera and hold her hand. At this point, he was surprised she hadn't mentioned a boyfriend left behind in the city. She was smart, funny, adventurous, and beautiful. She was the complete package, as far as he could tell. And for the next week, he was going to spend lots of time with her.

His eyes trailed to her full red lips which were slicked with a clear lip gloss. And he had to admit he was a sucker for brown eyes. His normal choice in women was petite, slender, and of the high maintenance variety, but Vera was the opposite in every way: tall and curvy, with minimal makeup. She didn't need much to enhance her attributes and the smattering of freckles across the bridge of her nose, well, let's just say he wanted to count them, which meant he'd be very, very close to her.

The saw swung comfortably from his hand and Uncle Frank was pointing to a tree. They had found *the one.*

He steered Vera toward the row.

"Can you make it through there? The snow looks about eight inches deep." She gave him a warm smile. "If you fall, I'm coming down with you, so it's all good."

"A tumble with you in the snow." He grinned and liked the way her eyes crinkled with laughter.

"Reminds me of this morning when you were holding me up."

"Seems we have a job on this vacation: Make sure you don't connect to any hard surfaces like the ground—and I'll do the same for you." He tucked her arm into his side and they slowly made their way down the row to Georgia and Uncle Frank.

Georgia had her cell phone out and was taking pictures of the tree. "Hey, you two slowpokes. Get in front of the tree so I can take a picture."

"Mom," Vera groaned. *A picture with her and Tony wasn't necessary. It wouldn't need to be preserved for all eternity in some old photo album.*

Georgia waved her hand and with a laugh requested, "Indulge me, please?"

Uncle Frank took her phone and said, "Get in the picture. I want one of you with Vera and Tony."

He stepped back and said, "Smile."

After a few clicks, Tony hobbled away from Vera. "Your turn."

"Tony, can you take a couple of me and Mom?"

"Sure."

Georgia glanced at Tony's foot. "What happened to you?"

"It's not a big deal. I just twisted it. But it will be fine."

Uncle Frank clapped a hand on his shoulder. "Should we swing by the emergency room?"

"Nah. Really, it's fine. Don't give it another thought."

A moment later, another tree-chopping customer came along and volunteered to take a picture of the four of them.

"What a nice family you have." She held up the phone. "Say PIZZA!"

They clowned around a few more minutes before it was time to cut the tree down. Vera knelt on the ground and looked at Tony.

"Let me show you how it's done."

He crossed his arms over his midsection and grinned. "Yup. It's good practice for when I have kids someday. We'll buy one cut." He grumbled, but it was in a good-natured way. He could see the benefits of taking the family out for this annual event.

With a few strokes of the saw on the front and then back of the trunk, the tree was falling. Everyone gathered around and grabbed a branch to drag it back up the hill.

Tony's limp was almost gone. It was good he wasn't hurt too badly, but would they still get that sleigh ride she had mentioned?

Once they got back to the overhang, one of the guys took

the tree and slid it through the netting machine and deposited it in the back of Frank's truck.

Georgia said, "Would you two like to take a sleigh ride now?"

Vera looked at her mom and Frank. "I thought we could all go together." She glanced over her shoulder. "There's a two-seater and a four-seater."

"I think we're going to head home, but you and Tony should go." She tucked her hand in the crook of Uncle Frank's arm. "We have a few other things to do."

"But what about stopping at Trim A Tree for our annual ornament?"

Georgia told Frank, "We never miss a year of getting something new for the tree."

Frank looked at Vera. "We'll meet you there after we finish my errand. I need to pick something up before dinner tonight. Say, in about an hour?"

Tony took Vera's hand. "Sounds great. See you in a bit." He tugged her toward the small food stand, where people were buying insulated cups of hot cocoa. "I get the feeling they want to spend a bit of time alone. And you promised me a ride in the sleigh."

"I did. I had forgotten how much all of these traditions meant to me." They waited in line for cocoa. "Are you enjoying yourself?"

"More than I thought I would. I've never been a huge fan of the holidays. After my parents died, the magic was gone. Uncle Frank did his best, but two guys bumbling around, trying to bake cookies when neither of us had a clue was tough. We resorted to slice and bakes."

"From the looks of him cooking this morning, I'd say he got better. But the question is did you?'

"I can feed myself but never did master the art of baking."

She ordered their hot cocoa with extra marshmallows and then said, "Guess what we're doing tomorrow?"

He pretended to shudder. "Baking cookies?"

"We are, and I promise it will be the highlight of the week."

"Only if I can sample as we go."

They strolled to the horse and carriage, which stood waiting for its next passengers. "That's half the fun of baking." She leaned away from him and said, "You look like a gingerbread man connoisseur."

"I've eaten my share but I don't know if I can bake them."

"To get things warmed up, why don't we volunteer to make dinner tonight? What's your specialty?"

Tony's brow furrowed.

"Does that look mean you have so many, you can't decide, or are you trying to choose the one thing that won't give us all food poisoning?"

He bumped her shoulder. "Since we're in New England, is there a good place to get seafood?"

She almost choked on her cocoa. "Of course there is. What are you thinking?"

"Lobster mac and cheese with a green salad and wine."

She smacked her lips. "I'll take care of the salad and dessert and we'll pick out the wine together."

He held up his hand to give her a high five. "I'm beginning to see the real value in teamwork. You'll do half the dishes, too."

Over her shoulder, she said, "That's still open for negotiations."

She stepped into the sleigh and slid across the seat. Once Tony was sitting, she pulled the colorful quilt over their legs. The driver snapped the reins and the horse eased the sleigh forward. They rode up the hill and were going around the perimeter of the tree farm. Tony put his arm around her shoulders to keep them both a little warmer from the cool breeze that kicked up.

"I never knew there was this much land to the farm." They rode in silence for a few minutes.

She sipped her cocoa.

He took his glove off. "You have a whipped cream moustache."

She ran her tongue over her top lip.

"Let me." He leaned in closer.

Her heart skipped. Was he going to kiss her? Did she want him to? *Yes.*

Using his thumb, he wiped the cream off her lip and dried it on his pants. "There. You're ready for the world of ornament shopping now."

Had he felt that zing? She looked away from him, hiding the unexpected rush of color on her cheeks.

The air was heavy with unspoken words. She cleared her throat. "This is fun."

Less than ten minutes later the sleigh pulled back around to their starting point. As far as she was concerned, the ride was way too short and not what she had expected.

Tony got down and held out his hand to help her. She took it.

"In case I trip?" She felt the need to explain the gesture.

As they walked to her car, he didn't release her hand. He said, "We haven't had the best track record the last two days with slips and trips."

"Ready for the next part of the tradition?" she asked.

"Can't wait." His eyes twinkled. "This really is the best Christmas I've had so far."

5

$\mathcal{T}$rim A Tree was always something Vera looked forward to. Not that she didn't visit the charming shop other times, but on tree day it was extra special. When she was little, she remembered coming here with her parents; these trips were some of her fondest memories of her father. The older she got, the more she realized there hadn't been enough time with him. Shaking off the melancholy, she parked her car right out front. Frank's truck was a few spaces down.

"What's your favorite kind of ornament?"

Tony looked at her. The corners of his eyes crinkled. "Round ones?"

Her hand flew to her throat in mock horror. "Please tell me you've shopped for special ornaments before today?"

"Sorry, department stores and boxes filled with twenty assorted ornaments is all I've done." He held his hands approximately three feet apart. "Fake tree and this tall."

With a vigorous shake of her head, she announced, "You're in for a treat. This place has everything. Glass balls, ornaments made from shells and bits of wood and, well, you'll see. And you *must* pick out one. It's tradition."

He tapped his index finger to his forehead. "I got it. Yes ma'am."

With a laugh, they walked up the steps. He kept an eye on her. She placed a hand lightly on his arm.

"You don't need to worry," he said. "My ankle feels better."

She pulled open the door and grinned. "Are you ready to feast your eyes on the most beautiful decorations you've ever seen?"

"I hope this little adventure lives up to your buildup."

He reached around her and pulled the door wider. She didn't move, waiting for his answer.

"After you."

VERA'S EYES sparkled when she talked about all of the ornaments as they walked up and down rows of decorated trees, some with a theme and some a hodgepodge. He liked those the best. The blend of colors and textures created an eclectic beauty. He never liked the perfect, themed trees Uncle Frank had done every year. The personality of the family wasn't on display.

She picked up angel ornaments with feathers for wings, handblown glass bulbs, wreath ornaments made from twigs and berries, to name a few. Most of the decorations she gravitated toward were handcrafted by local artisans. He could see why. The workmanship was exquisite.

"Have you seen anything you like yet?"

Joking, he said, "I can only select one, so I have to take my time and make my choice carefully since this will set the tone for years to come."

Her eyes were round and held a serious look. "I understand. Do you feel drawn to a specific type?"

He strolled to the front window display. "I like the ornaments that are representative of the town." He held up a gazebo with a tiny tree under its rafters. "This is nice."

"But does it call to you?" She picked up a glass angel ornament. "This is beautiful. She's a wish angel."

He was intrigued. "What's a wish angel? Like when you blow out birthday candles?"

She handed the ornament to him. In the center, the angel was holding a star outlined in gold. It was beautiful. He knew he would purchase this for her, but as a surprise.

"My dad used to tell me to make a Christmas wish. The one that is deep in your heart, not for something material, but what you long for."

"Did you make a wish this year?"

Her eyes were bright. "I did. When we drove through town."

"What was it?"

She looked away as if he could peer into her and discover her heartfelt wish. "I can't tell you that."

The spell was broken and the moment lost.

Vera looked around.

"I'm going to see how Mom and Frank are doing selecting their new ornament, and also let them know we're cooking tonight."

She strolled down the aisle and he took the angel ornament to the counter and purchased it before she got back. Then he'd find another one to purchase for the tree.

VERA AND TONY stepped into the crisp afternoon air. Flurries were drifting down from the scattered clouds despite the still-shining sun.

"I can't believe someone bought the last angel ornament." She jammed her hands into her coat pockets. "But I'm happy with the pewter maple leaf I found, and the replica of the town tree is perfect."

He opened her car door but she didn't get in. "I think it is a good first step," he said. "Almost as if acknowledging I'm ready for Christmas since I had a hand in buying two trees for the day. That is a record."

"Mom was secretive when it came to what she and Frank bought. I can't wait to see when we decorate the tree tonight."

"Is there someplace nearby we can get wine? And I was thinking we'd pick up a bottle of Prosecco for dessert."

"We'll swing by the liquor store first and then the market." She got behind the wheel, closed the door, and pointed to the passenger seat.

When he was buckled, she said, "Let's do a slow tour of the rest of Main Street to check out decorations. The Library Cat Bookstore window is always a treat to window shoppers. Heather Murphy owns the bookstore, and she knows how to draw customers inside."

"It sounds like it's better to stroll down the street than drive."

She flashed him a grin. "That's on tomorrow's plan, oh and caroling. We're going."

She hoped her excitement was contagious. Tony needed to have more fun. He was far too serious and it was Christmas, the time to let your inner child out to play.

"You keep adding to our days and we're going to run out of hours to get everything squeezed in."

"Don't you worry. I learned from the best on how to extract every bit of holiday fun from the week before Christmas until New Year's Day."

"Your mom?"

"After my dad passed away, she and I had a new adventure, big or small, every single day. This is a magical time of year and Mom helped me believe that anything is possible."

"Even starting a new business in your hometown?"

She watched the road ahead, but Tony's question cemented her decision. "Yes. Tomorrow I'm going to talk to

Mom about moving home for a while until I can sell my condo. I'll find a place here and of course set up my business."

"You've set a new course of action. I envy you."

"Jump in; the water's warm." She glanced at him. "I thought you were happy living in the city?"

"Let's just say you're not the only one contemplating a crossroad."

"Tony, remember anything really is possible. You just need to believe in yourself."

"Thanks. That means a lot and I'm really glad, despite the circumstances, you picked me up off the side of the road."

She snorted. "It's a good thing for us that Tom vouched for you. Otherwise you'd have become a six-foot popsicle."

THE DINING ROOM table was set. The salad greens were tossed and Tony had just checked on the main dish, macaroni in a rich cheese sauce with chunks of fresh lobster. A plate of frosted sugar cookies would cap the meal as they decorated the tree.

Vera walked into the living room. Mollie was snoozing in her favorite spot, oblivious to the excitement going on around her, and Vera had to admit Frank's tree looked pretty with white twinkle lights. From the street, people could see it through the picture window. Maybe tomorrow she could convince Tony to build a snowman with her. Heck, maybe a snow family with all the white stuff that had accumulated. It was still snowing, too.

She heard him come up behind her.

"It's big, but it does look good."

She gestured to the stacked boxes. "I think they've combined ornaments. Some of those boxes, I've never seen before."

He knelt down. "This one was from my parents."

She looked out the window as he wiped his cheeks with the back of his hand. He cleared his throat. "I need to check on dinner."

Mom and Frank were coming down the stairs. She knew from their conversation it was the last two boxes of ornaments. Even Frank was happy they had come to the end.

"Vera, you look pretty tonight," Mom remarked as she set down the box that held the angel.

"I changed. My jeans were damp from being outside. Is that a new sweater?"

"Traditions. Frank and I each bought tree trimming sweaters."

He put his arm around her shoulders. "Your mother has introduced me to the magic of the season. This is my very first Christmas sweater."

Tony joined them. "What's going on in here?" He pointed to Frank and Mom's matching sweaters.

She held up a finger and scooted out of the room, returning with two bags. "For you." She handed one to Tony and one to Vera. With a gleam in her eye, she said, "For tonight."

Looking inside, Tony broke into a wide grin. "My very first sweater. It's a Christmas tree." He pulled it on over his head. "What's yours?"

Vera held up a red sweater with two reindeer dancing across the front.

With a hoot, he said, "That is so great. We have trees, snowman, candy canes, and now the reindeer. We need a selfie." He pulled his cell phone out and gestured for everyone to gather around.

Tony, Vera, Mom, and Frank lined up in front of the fireplace and grinned.

He took a look at the snaps and showed everyone. "I think we got a few good ones."

The stove timer buzzed.

"That's our cue. Dinner is ready."

FRANK PUSHED BACK his chair and patted his belly. "Thank you for making a delicious dinner."

Mom stood to clear the table.

Vera took the plate from her hand. "Relax. Tony and I have this."

They cleaned the table and set the plate of cookies in the middle. Tony brought in clean wine glasses and the Prosecco.

Frank said, "Before you open that, can you have a seat?"

Vera looked at Tony. He raised an eyebrow and she turned back to Frank.

HER MOUTH FELL open as he pushed back from the table. As if in slow motion, he dropped to one knee and took her mom's hand.

"Georgia, this is not the typical way to ask a very special woman a question, but it wouldn't seem right if Vera and Tony weren't with us."

Vera took Tony's hand and squeezed tight. He wasn't going to propose, was he?

"We both have been through tough times that made us stronger. The day I met you, I knew I had found the woman I would love for the rest of my life. Georgia Davis, will you marry me and allow me the honor of spending the rest of our days together?"

He pulled a diamond ring from his pocket and waited until she said, "Yes!" before sliding it on her finger. He pulled her from the chair into his arms.

She pecked his lips. "You've made me so happy."

Vera could see her mom was crying and she felt her heart slow. How could she and Tony put a damper on things now, when the relationship had just accelerated?

She felt pressure on her hand. Tony tugged her out of the chair and toward the kitchen. This was not a moment they should continue to intrude on.

Once they were in the kitchen, Vera whispered, "So now what are we going to do?"

"I have no idea." He put his arms around her and hugged her close.

And she liked it.

6

She stepped from the warmth of his arms and forced a smile.

"We need to get back in there. There's a tree to decorate."

"Are you going to be alright? Uncle Frank's proposal was not what I expected tonight."

"Me either, but now is not the right time for me to have a pointed conversation with Mom. You'll need to talk with your uncle. They are moving way too fast."

"But you have to admit that was one heck of a proposal. I wouldn't have guessed my uncle was such a romantic."

"Vera, Tony, we're ready to decorate the tree." Mom's voice drifted in to the kitchen.

"Hold on, Mom. I need to let Mollie out first."

Hearing her name, Mollie trotted to the back door and waited for it to open as if by magic. Vera watched her run into the snow, do her business, and hightail it back inside where it was warm and comfy. Mollie made a detour to her bowl for a snack and a drink and then meandered back toward the living room.

Tony said, "Let's try to keep the conversation away from the impending nuptials and stay focused on the task at hand." He brushed a lock of hair out of Vera's eyes. The simple gesture was sweet and when she looked up, she could see longing in his. Or did they reflect what was in hers?

"Um. Well, let's." She pointed to the living room.

Tony let her lead the way. "After you."

THE FIRST THING Tony noticed when they entered the room was Uncle Frank's smile. It was as if it began at his toes and was so powerful, it burst through the top of his head. How could he have a conversation and tactfully tell this man he should slow down this romance? It was witnessing the looks between Georgia and Uncle Frank that he felt a gut punch. What he wouldn't give to be on the receiving and giving end of a similar connection. It was palpable between the newly engaged couple.

"Tony, you should be the first one to hang your new ornament on the tree." Vera handed him the small brown paper bag that bore the logo from the Trim a Tree shop.

"You should. After all, this is your home. I'm just a guest."

Georgia walked to him and placed her fingers on his hand. "Nonsense. You're family." She pointed to the tree. "Pick a spot and let's get this party started."

The expectation of just the right placement weighed heavy on him.

Vera quickly lost patience with waiting for him to choose. "It's a large tree and you can always move it."

He placed it at his eye level in the middle, it was a replica of the town tree. He said "Ta-da" and stepped aside. "How's that?"

"Perfect." Vera gave him a heart-thumping smile. There had to be something in the air. He loved dating, but in meeting Vera, things were different. The pulse racing, heart hammering, and the way her perfume teased his senses was putting him off kilter.

With each box that was opened and ornaments hung, there were stories of Vera in school, making orange juice lid ornaments complete with her photo, teeth missing and beaming, and a jar's worth of glitter on front and back. All of these were proudly hung on the tree.

Uncle Frank opened a box and handed him a popsicle angel. "Do you remember this, Tony?"

"I made it." He took it carefully, afraid the decades-old ornament would break apart in his hand. "I can't believe you kept it."

With a twinkle in his eye, Uncle Frank gestured to the box. "I kept all the ornaments you made. Go ahead and add what you want to the tree."

"But—"

Georgia was nodding. "This is so much fun and we're getting to know each other even more as we unearth the multitude of treasures."

Vera peered into the box and pulled out a construction paper Santa, complete with cotton balls for a beard. Holding it, she crossed the room to a box with her name on it and withdrew a Mrs. Santa. She said, "These have to go on the tree. For years, Mrs. Claus has been wondering what the heck happened to her hubby, and it's clear he was hiding."

Georgia took the paper ornaments and hung them on the tree. "When all the kids in Vera's class were following the directions to make Santa, she thought it wasn't fair that his wife was overlooked. As usual, she blazed her own path and made the Mrs." She tapped her chin with her finger. "Now that I think of it, you never did make Santa. All these years, we've just had her."

"It looks like they belong together." Tony's eyes sought Vera's. "It's official. They'll be together forever now."

Was he talking about a child's simple ornament or something more?

"Who's up for more cookies?" Vera asked. "Cocoa or tea?"

"Vera, I'm going to hold off on more cookies until tomorrow. It's been quite the day and after we clean up, I think we're going to head to bed." Georgia began to stack boxes inside of boxes.

At the same time, Tony and Vera said, "We'll clean this up."

Georgia looked at Frank. "Do you want a snack?"

He patted his belly. "I need to watch my weight. I have a tux to fit into at some point."

Tony sensed that Vera's heart dropped at the mention of a tux. Did this mean they had set the date? He wasn't going to ask tonight. Tomorrow, he'd get Uncle Frank alone and Vera would talk to Georgia. That was all they could do.

"Goodnight Uncle Frank. Goodnight Georgia."

Vera kissed her mom's cheek and murmured, "Sleep well."

As the happy couple ascended the stairs, Georgia called out, "See you at eight for breakfast."

Vera plopped on the couch and dropped her head on the back. She groaned. "Can you believe they're already making wedding plans? What's the rush?" She looked at Tony. "Why don't you seem that upset?"

"There is nothing I can do about it tonight." He stacked a few more boxes and sat next to her. "Did you see their faces? The way they were looking at each other. Pure joy."

"That doesn't mean they can't slow down and wait a while to get hitched. It's not like they're old, with one foot on a banana peel, sliding into home plate at the pearly gates."

"Interesting mental image." He patted her leg. "It's late and like I said, tomorrow is a new day. Do you want to talk to your mom right after breakfast or wait awhile?"

Vera sat up and took a snowman cookie from the plate. She nibbled around the edge before taking a bigger bite. She munched and her face was screwed up in concentration.

"After breakfast, you and Frank can go check on your

truck, leaving me here with Mom. I'll talk to her while you're gone, and you can get the lowdown from your uncle at the same time. Then when you get back, you and I will take off into town, leaving them to talk and agree to put the potential wedding on hold."

She polished off the last of her cookie and grinned. Crumbs clung to the corner of her mouth. He brushed them off while thinking he'd rather kiss her lush lips instead.

"Tony? Do you have a better idea?"

He shook his head. "That's as good as any plan. But one question; what do we do if they get so mad they stop talking to us?"

"Hm. We need to be really careful with what we say and how it's said so it doesn't come off sounding like I don't like Frank or you don't like Mom."

"Your mom is great. It's easy to see why Uncle Frank loves her."

Vera perked up. "Thanks, and Frank is sweet to Mom. I can see the attraction, and she's been alone a long time. It's been almost twenty-two years since my dad died."

"Has she dated much since?"

"Frank is the first guy I know of; that's why I'm worried. How can she possibly know he's the one if she has nothing to compare him to?"

"Uncle Frank had lots of friends, but no one special either."

"I mean, when I meet the guy I want to spend my life with, I'll know. I've certainly kissed enough frogs."

"I hear ya. I've kissed enough frogettes to last me a lifetime."

Vera laughed, "Is that even a real word? Frogette?"

"No. I made it up since I wasn't sure how to compare to kissing frogs."

Vera hooted with laughter. "You're so funny. I'm glad

we're going through this together and when all this is settled, we'll be related." Her laughter died.

They'd be together for holidays, and eventually Vera would have a man in her life. What if Tony didn't like him? That was going to be hard to swallow. She deserved the best.

He asked, "What will we be to each other? Will you be like my cousin or something?"

"Sounds about right."

She nodded her head. "Well. I'm just going to finish cleaning up the glasses and cookies and head up." She stood and crossed the room. "See you in the morning."

"I'll help."

"No, there isn't much to do and it will only take a few minutes." She bopped her head toward the stairs. "Goodnight."

She waited until she heard Tony's bedroom door shut before she walked into the kitchen. She needed to be alone. So many feelings threatened to overwhelm her. Mom engaged. Frank living here. Meeting Tony. She didn't even want to delve too deeply into the way she felt when they were together. Today had been more fun than she had ever had on any first date. Not that this was a date, she quickly reminded herself. Even if they had done date kinds of things. Tony was easy to talk to and he made her laugh. It was too bad her mind kept drifting back to his eyes and dark hair and the smile that could make any girl's knees get weak.

She finished loading the dishwasher and fixed a cup of sleepytime tea with honey. She would need all the help she could get tonight.

"Come on, Mollie. Time for bed."

7

*F*or the second day in a row wonderful smells woke Vera from a sound sleep. Mollie was already sitting next to the door, waiting to be let out of the bedroom.

Vera dressed in a long red turtleneck sweater that covered her rear and leggings that had Santa faces all over them. It was two days until Christmas and she wasn't going to work, so why not be comfy? After a quick bathroom stop, she was ready for the day.

She still didn't know what she was going to say after Tony and Frank left, but she was confident she'd find the right words and tone. She didn't want to hurt her mom, but better she be honest now to save Mom potential heartbreak later.

She descended the front stairs so she could swing through the living room and turn on the tree lights. Why wait until it was dark before enjoying it? To her surprise, it was already on. Mom must have taken care of it. She strolled into the kitchen, taking note of the baking supplies spread out on the dining room table. It looked like the elf factory was going into full production today.

"Good morning everyone." She made a beeline for the coffee pot and snagged a piece of bacon on the way.

"Morning, Vera." Tony walked to her and took the other half of her bacon. "You need to share the good stuff." He winked.

"Someone slept well last night." Her tone was light and teasing.

"Like a rock. You?"

Mom and Frank were putting the finishing touches on plates of scrambled eggs, bacon, and cinnamon rolls. Vera took two plates and carried them to the table.

Over breakfast, they talked of plans for the day.

Tony asked, "Uncle Frank, any chance you can take me down to the garage after breakfast? I want to check on the truck and see if it's ready."

"Give them a call."

"Well, I also wanted to do a little shopping and thought maybe you could help me."

"Why didn't you say so." Frank glanced at Mom. "Do you need anything while we're out?"

Mom said, "No. I'm on the fence about what to fix for dinner."

"Mom, I'll take KP duty. You made breakfast and by the looks of the dining room, you're baking cookies today too."

"I thought it'd be fun if we all circle back and make a couple of batches this afternoon. Then after dinner, we'll go to the village green for caroling."

Tony piped up, "Sounds good to me."

Vera sipped her juice. "Me too."

THE HOUSE WAS QUIET. Mom had walked Frank out to his truck, which would have been cute if Vera hadn't been about to broach the very touchy subject of the engagement. Mollie was cavorting in the backyard, enjoying the freedom that came with a fenced in backyard. Her move to Dickens would be good for Mollie too. Well, that's if Mom would be receptive to her moving back after this conversation.

Mom whisked in the back door, color high in her cheeks, and Vera was sure it wasn't the winter weather that put the pink there.

"Isn't he just the sweetest man you've ever met?"

"He's pretty great."

Mom gave her a sharp look. "Vera, do you have something on your mind?"

She could never get anything past her mom. "Can we talk for a bit?"

She pulled two kitchen chairs out from the table and sat down. Mom sat across from her.

"Mom." She placed her hands palm side down on the table. "Why didn't you tell me that you were dating Frank? Instead you led me to believe a woman named Fran had moved in with you."

She waved her hand. "I never said a woman, although I do recall dropping the K in his name."

"Why? You knew I'd come home and find out eventually. Especially since he's living here."

"In my defense, I didn't expect you to come home in the middle of the night. Imagine my surprise when headlights flitted across the living room."

"You're avoiding the question. Why didn't you tell me about Frank?"

"I didn't think you'd understand. Or accept that I was moving on. I've been waiting for you to be ready, and when I met him, it was like a brilliant light was turned on in a dark room that was full of plants. I began to grow outside of the walls I had built around myself. You're living in the city, and it's time for me to have a life."

"But how well do you know him? Do you think you should rush into marriage? Live together a little longer and if at this time next year you still think marrying Frank is the right thing to do, you'll have my full support."

Mom sat up straight in her chair, her face a mask.

"First of all, you seem to have forgotten that I'm not some naïve schoolgirl with her first crush. When I met your dad, I knew within an hour that he was the man I would marry. Less than six months later, we said I do. Six months." She let that sink in for a long minute.

"I didn't know that," Vera said after she thought about what her mother had just said. "I always thought you took your time, got to know each other."

"You didn't ask, either. I guess you assumed. But love happens like that sometimes. It just jumps into your heart and won't let go."

"But Frank and you…" Her voice trailed off.

"Our relationship has evolved slowly. We were friends first, then started to date, and we love spending time together. With his business, he can work from anywhere and travels occasionally and with me writing cookbooks, as long as I have a kitchen, I can create and work."

"Mom, are you sure this is the right thing to do for your future?"

She took Vera's hands. "Yes, it is. But there is something you should take to heart. When the man walks into your life who makes you laugh, not that fake polite laugh we all do, but the kind that warms you from the inside out, he's the guy you keep. Don't think just making a heartfelt wish does all the work for you. Open your eyes before your wish leaves town."

"What are you talking about?"

"Tony. All the signs are there, but you need to see them for yourself." She squeezed Vera's hands. "Trust me. I know what I'm talking about. I got lucky. I've met two men in my life who made me really laugh. Your dad and now Frank."

Mom left Vera sitting at the kitchen table with much to

think about. Vera wondered how it was going with Tony and Frank.

"UNCLE FRANK, what happened to your house?" They were leaving the garage and headed down to Dorrit's Diner for a coffee. It was as good a place as any to have the dreaded conversation.

"I've still got it. Any interest in moving to town? It'd make a great home to raise a family."

"In order to have a family, I need to start with a wife."

Uncle Frank gave him a side-eye.

"I know what you're thinking and I just met Vera. How do I know we'll be compatible long-term? I mean, she's smart, pretty, and has that amazing laugh that is infectious, but it takes a long time to really get to know if someone will stick."

Tony opened the door to the diner and they took a booth. The high sides were perfect for keeping their conversation from becoming part of the telephone game for the locals.

"But I didn't ask you to come out and talk about me and Vera. I wanted to talk about Georgia." He held up two fingers to the waitress for coffee. He didn't seem to notice Uncle Frank never even mentioned Vera.

She came over and poured. After asking if they needed anything else, she left them.

"Isn't Georgia the most amazing woman you've ever met? Talk about the complete package. She just does it for me." He put air quotes around *does it*.

"How long have you been dating?" Tony added cream and sugar to his overly dark coffee.

"I see where this is going. You think I'm rushing into something and I need to pull back. Slow it down and make sure I love her and she really does love me before we take the plunge."

Tony nodded. "Something like that."

"I appreciate your concern, but there are a few things you need to understand and maybe then you'll see why she is so important to me and why I'm going to marry her."

Tony listened while Frank extolled Georgia's virtues and how he had never been this happy.

"Do you know she is the only woman I've ever wanted to propose to?"

"But you dated a lot of nice women. I met a few."

"You're right, but they all were missing something and I never wanted to settle for less than a woman who would touch my soul."

"And Georgia does?"

"In the last two years, I've laughed and lived more than I did in the last thirty. She is smart and kind and challenges me to get out of my comfort zone on a regular basis, and I hope I do the same for her. But I respect the heck out of her. Raising Vera on her own, writing cookbooks—which, I know you've only had her delicious breakfast foods, but she is an amazing cook. Her books are bestsellers."

"I had no idea." Tony stared into his cup. He had to wonder how Vera's conversation was going with her mom.

"Tony, what about you? Have you found someone who you want to spend a lifetime making memories with? Vera perhaps?"

"Uncle Frank, we just met. It's been, what? Three days. No one falls in love in just three days."

"Sometimes it only takes three minutes." He leaned back in the booth. "I can't remember the last time I've seen you look so relaxed and carefree. Since you've been here, you don't look like you're my brother instead of my nephew."

"Are you saying I'm an old fart?"

"No. What I'm saying is maybe it's time you let go and allow your heart to make a wish for love."

With a laugh, Tony said, "Now I know you're in love. Look at you being all mushy."

Uncle Frank perked up. "I wear it well, don't I."

"You're one thousand percent sure Georgia is the only woman for you? I can't talk you into slowing down and, say, get married a year from now?"

"Not a chance. I've been to more June weddings than I'd care to remember, and we want to get married the fourth Saturday in June." He grinned. "Can I count on you to be my best man?"

"I'd be honored."

VERA WAS SITTING on the front porch with Mollie by her side when Frank parked his truck in the driveway. Tony jogged up the front steps after parking his own truck on the street.

"Are you taking Mollie for a walk?"

"I am. Want to come?"

"Yes." He knew she was anxious to share what they each had learned. As he scratched Mollie's ears, he asked, "Hey girl, ready to stretch your legs?"

Mollie stood up, and it seemed as if she was smiling. Her tail was beating the side of his leg.

"Someone is excited." He took her leash.

Once on the sidewalk, they strolled toward the center of town. Vera seemed to be waiting for him to spill his guts.

"They love each other. Your mom and my uncle."

"We already knew that." Vera pointed down a new side street. "Let's go that way."

"Uncle Frank said your mom is the first woman he's ever wanted to marry." He kicked a ball of snow. "He asked me to be his best man."

"And you said?"

"Of course I said yes. I love him, and he's done so much for me."

"I guess that's that."

"He offered me his house. He hasn't sold it yet."

"That was nice."

Could this conversation be any more stilted?

"Vera, if your mom told you similar things to what Uncle Frank said, we need to let this go. Be happy they found someone. We know how hard that is."

He wasn't going to divulge all of what his uncle had said. It was nuts for him to have implied he had strong feelings for Vera. No matter what he thought, nobody falls in love in three days.

Vera came to a stop on the back side of the village green.

"Have you made your Christmas wish yet?"

"Do you really believe in wishes?"

She pointed to the tree. "Close your eyes and silently make a wish."

She closed her eyes and stood there, quiet. He did the same.

When he opened them again, she was looking at him.

She smiled. "Good. Now, let's take Mollie home. There is a baking lesson in your future."

8

*V*era wiped a smudge of flour from Tony's face with a chuckle. "I see you've immersed yourself in cookie baking."

His finger trailed down her cheek, adding a smear to her face. "You look good in white." He held up his finger. "Flour, I meant."

She grabbed a damp towel and wiped her face off. Easing the ping in her heart, she laughed it off. "It's a good thing we're baking thumbprint cookies but haven't gotten to the jam part yet. Otherwise you might have raspberry jam on your face too."

He put up his hands in self-defense. "Wait! I was just having a little fun." The twinkle in his eye betrayed his playful side. "So, what do we do next? Scoop these on the sheet and put them in the oven, and when do we put the jam on them?"

"Patience, take a small amount of dough in your hand. About a teaspoonful and roll it into a ball, making sure you can't see any cracks in the dough."

He had a heaping spoonful and began to roll the dough to golf-ball size. She touched his hand.

"Hold on there. That is a little too big. The cookies need to be roughly the same size to bake evenly." She pinched off a hunk from one side. "Try that."

Tony rerolled the dough, checking to see how Vera's cookies were shaping up. She had lined up four little balls to his one.

"How's this?" He held up a perfectly shaped ball.

"Great. Follow the spacing and make more. Once they're ready, we'll use our thumb to make an impression in them and fill the hole with slightly warmed raspberry jam."

"What other kinds are we making?" He began to roll his next cookie.

"Apricot?"

He wrinkled his nose. "What about the apple jam your mom has in the fridge? I'll bet that would be really good in these."

"I never thought about that. The caramel flavor in the jam would be tasty with this cookie. I'll get some and we can do half and half."

"By the way, do you think your mom and my uncle are upset with us?"

"No. Why?"

"They disappeared pretty quick when it was time to make these cookies."

"Mom has already done a ton of baking, but these are my favorites to make. I'm sure she saved them for me and you." She looked up and grinned. "Are you having fun?"

"Yeah, but I'll have more fun when I'm eating some of these. Do they have to cool completely before I get a sample?"

"Trust me; you're going to want them to cool. That jam is going to be hot after being in the oven. I'm going to suggest about ten minutes after they come out, you can try one."

With a snort, he said, "I'm trying at least two—one of each kind. Care to join me?"

"Only if you make the coffee." She finished the last of the

balls and moved the cookie sheets closer. "Come stand next to me."

Tony walked around the island.

She took his hand and positioned his thumb over the center of the dough ball.

"Gently, make an indent about halfway down and pull your thumb straight out."

He made a slight indent. "Like that?"

She took his hand and guided it. "No. Sink your thumb in to almost the bottom of your nail. Being careful to not push too hard and crack the dough."

She watched as he moved to the next ball. "While you finish that, I'll warm the jam."

She could feel his eyes follow her to the microwave. She warmed the two flavors of jam and wondered why she had never thought to use the apple. Over her shoulder, she said, "I might just make a baker out of you yet. The idea of the apple jam was genius."

"We haven't tasted it yet."

Baking with Tony had become very intimate. She had never made Christmas cookies with any of her previous boyfriends, but she was having fun and Tony seemed to be enjoying the entire process. He was a quick learner. Baking was precise, not like making a meal where a little of this and that tossed in and it could still turn out fabulous.

"I'm done."

The microwave dinged and she grabbed the glass bowls by their edges and moved them to the counter, releasing them with a clatter. "Those are hot."

He turned on the cold water and held her hands under the tap.

From under her lashes, she studied him. He really was a sweet guy.

"Thanks. They're better now."

He handed her a dry towel. "Potholders are where?"

She pointed to a drawer next to the stove. "I should have thought about using them in the first place."

"I'll get them. You start filling the cookies." He gave her a wink. "How long do they have to bake? I'm getting hungry."

She tossed the towel at him. "I'm going to ask Santa to bring you a box full of patience."

He ducked. "There's an old saying: Patience is a virtue, possess it if you can. Seldom found in women, never found in men. Or I think that is how it goes."

"Are you telling me that I have more patience than you?" She bobbed her head. "Very observant."

Teasing, he said, "I just lumped myself in a box."

"And just when I thought you were different from all the other guys in the world." She thrust a spoon in his direction. "Start putting the jam in."

"You're so focused."

"I'm not going to be the reason you don't get an afternoon snack."

"Are there food vendors at the village green tonight?" His stomach grumbled right on cue.

She burst out laughing. "Don't worry. You won't starve."

MOLLIE CAME TROTTING into the front hallway and sat down.

Tony knelt down to pet her. "I don't think you're going with us tonight. It's pretty cold out there." He leaned in closer and whispered in her ear, "Snuggle up in your blanket and stay warm. I'll tell you all about it when we get home."

She gave him a lick on his cheek and wandered into the living room to hop up on the couch as if she understood every word he had said.

Vera came in and was wrapping a red plaid blanket scarf around her neck. She peeked in the other room to see what Mollie was doing. "I'm surprised she isn't asking to go with us."

"She came out but I told her it was really cold and I'd fill her in on all the details when we got back. Heck, I'll take a picture of the tree and show her too."

Vera chuckled. "She does understand human as well as dog."

"Your mom and Uncle Frank said they'd be down in a minute or two. Then we can take off."

She looked him up and down. "Are you going to be warm enough?"

He patted his pockets. "Gloves and a hat." He waved his hand over her outfit. "You look warm."

"The key is the blanket scarf." She held out the corners. "I can wrap this around me and be really warm."

He noted it looked big enough for two and his mind did wander to getting close to her within the folds of the wool.

"Hey, did I lose you?"

He snapped out of his daydream. "Sorry. Thinking of a story I need to turn in."

Uncle Frank and Georgia took that moment to bustle into the foyer.

Georgia looped her arm through Vera's. "Are you two ready? I want us to get a good spot near the tree."

She and his uncle led the way, holding hands and talking about different outdoor decorations they wanted to get on sale after Christmas. He had never seen this side of Uncle Frank before, and it was nice.

VERA DISCOVERED it was easier to see Mom and Frank together since they had talked yesterday. Who was she to stand in their way of happiness and if she did, she'd be the loser. She wasn't going to risk putting a wedge between her and Mom.

As they walked, she stole a look at Tony. His bright green knit cap was pulled low on his head and she smothered a smile when she saw his gloves. They had huge

Mickey Mouse faces stitched on them. They looked vaguely familiar.

"Did you get those out of the closet?" She pointed to his hands.

"No. They're mine. Do you like them?"

"I do." Another zing of similarity.

He looped his arm through hers. "Just in case of ice." His eyes were bright as he tried to play it cool.

"Mom found her spot. Come on."

Their steps quickened as they grew closer to the growing crowd. Tony was absorbing the sights and throngs of people. *He fits in perfectly, small town life suits him.*

"Is the entire town here?"

"Pretty much. Dicken-ites love all holidays, but Christmas most of all." She grinned. "It kind of fits with the name of our town and all."

He drank in the sites. "It's something out of a Christmas card. Right down to the raised dais with Santa waiting until we're done singing."

"Then Santa will take his spot and the children can make their last wishes."

"Uncle Frank and I never went caroling."

He chimed in, "I'm sorry we missed this. I'm having the best time." He dropped a kiss on Mom's forehead.

"It'll be the first of many. Vera and I haven't missed one since she was born." Mom's eyes were misty. "It's nice being together to start a new tradition."

Vera glanced at the clock on the church steeple. "We have some time. Does anyone want a cup of hot cocoa?"

After agreeing it would hit the spot, Tony volunteered to go with her.

They strolled through the crowd of adults and children whose faces were filled with the excitement of seeing Santa. She knew they wouldn't be sleeping much tonight, with Christmas just around the corner.

"Tell me, have you enjoyed being immersed in the Davis family traditions?"

"I have. Next year, it will be the Davis-Barbee traditions of a blended family." He shoulder bumped her. "Is there something you'd like to do that you haven't yet?"

"Not really. We've been to Gridley's, Trim A Tree, the tea shop, and we've even taken a sleigh ride."

"What was the highlight?"

She gave him a toothy smile. "Can I say all of it? There has been something very special about this year."

"Could it be you've made a decision about your future? You're content with what will happen after the new year?"

"That plays a part in my happiness." She stopped short of telling Tony he was also a part of what had been different but nice about this year.

They ordered four cups of cocoa with whipped cream. They each took two cups and strolled back to Georgia and Frank.

The band struck up the first chords of a carol, and the combined voices of young and old melded. Everyone sang "O Christmas Tree, O Christmas Tree." After a few more songs, both silly and sentimental, they finished with "Silent Night."

The last strains hung in the air. Tony took that moment to announce, "I've been putting off telling you all, but I got an urgent email. I need to get back to the city tomorrow. Work thing."

Vera's mouth dropped open. She stammered, "Tomorrow is Christmas Eve. Can't it wait a couple of days?"

He dropped his gaze to the snow-covered grass, avoiding her eyes. "It can't. I'm sorry."

9

*T*ony spent a sleepless night. He still couldn't believe he had ruined the evening by saying he was leaving. If he stayed, he'd make a fool of himself. He got what Uncle Frank had said about the heart knowing what it wants. Tony had fallen in love with Vera. He silently agreed with her that this year had been special for him, and it was because of her. But he couldn't bear it if she rejected him.

These feelings were foreign to him. The only way to deal with them was to put space between the two of them. He was going to get Uncle Frank alone and explain the real reason for leaving. He would understand. Maybe.

Tony threw the last of his clothes in his duffel bag. There was a soft knock on the door.

"Come in."

Uncle Frank eased it open. "Do you have a minute?"

He waved his uncle inside.

"Care to tell me the real reason you're rushing out of town? I know it has nothing to do with work." He sat on the corner of the bed and gave him a hard look. "Your announcement caught everyone off guard."

He leaned against the dresser. "I'm sorry. I have to go."

"It's Christmas, and we have so much to celebrate. You haven't been home for a few years, always off someplace."

He hung his head. Should he speak freely and tell him why he was leaving, lest Uncle Frank think it had something to do with Georgia? Heck, he probably wouldn't be any happier when he found out it was because of Vera. His future step-daughter.

"What's weighing heavy on your mind?" He cocked his head. "I can sit here all day if necessary."

That was just like Uncle Frank, to wait him out, just like when he was a kid. Over the years, he had discovered it was easier to speak than wait. Frank Barbee was a very patient man.

"I can't be here, with Vera."

His brow arched. "Did you have an argument?"

"Nothing like that. If we had, this would be easier."

"You're using work as an excuse. There's no emergency, is there?"

"No. Unless you call throwing caution to the wind and losing my heart and wanting the girl across the hall." He sank to the wooden chair next to the dresser. "Remember when you told me you knew Georgia was the one for you?"

Uncle Frank nodded but didn't speak. He waited patiently.

"When she stopped alongside the road where I was broken down and apologized for not letting me get in her car, I was intrigued. But then she backed up and put her flashers on so that no one would hit me, I realized she had the biggest heart. Who does that for a complete stranger? That was it. I was a goner."

He hopped out of the chair and crossed to the window. "These last few days, spending time together, it's like we're on the same wavelength. It's easy to be with her and after the first day, I tried to tell myself I had discovered you can be friends with a woman." He snorted. "But who was I kidding?

I wanted so much more than that but she looks at me like a friend and soon to be a, well I don't know what, cousin or something."

"Why don't you tell her how you feel? Isn't it better than running away from the woman who might want to spend time with you? After all, you live in the same city."

"Which brings me to another hurdle. She wants to move back to Dickens and start a company so she can be close to her mom again. Small town life suits her."

Uncle Frank grew thoughtful. "I wonder why Georgia hasn't mentioned that to me?"

"Vera hasn't talked to her yet. And please keep that between us."

"I will. Why can't you live here? I've offered you the house. If you don't want to take it, I'll sell it to you at the family discount." He gave Tony a warm smile. "It'd be good to have you here too."

"I appreciate the offer, but it's better this way." He grabbed his duffel bag. "Walk me out?"

"I can't change your mind and at least get you to stay two more days?"

Tony shook his head and slung his bag over his shoulder. "It will only make it that much harder to leave." He stuck out his hand and Uncle Frank pulled him in for a bear hug.

"The door is always open, day or night."

"Thanks. I'll keep that in mind."

VERA SAT at the breakfast table long after Tony had said goodbye. The coffee in her mug was stone cold and even Mollie looked dejected, lying at her feet with her head resting on Vera's slipper.

Mom had asked Frank to run to the market for her and with a kiss on her cheek, he had gone out the front. She heard his truck rumble out of the drive. Its sound grew faint with the passing moments.

She thought about getting more coffee but decided she would rather sit and wallow. The house seemed empty with Tony gone. It had been only a few days and already she had grown accustomed to his presence.

Mom bustled into the kitchen and swiped Vera's mug from the table. Pouring the cold coffee down the drain, she refilled it and got a cup for herself. As soon as the chair slid across the floor, she said, "Spill it."

"What are you talking about?"

"Did you and Tony have words about Frank and me?"

She lifted her eyes and looked over Mom's head at the ceiling. "No. I mean, we talked about the situation and we agreed he'd talk to Frank and I'd talk to you. However, once we both realized how happy you were, we dropped it."

Mom laughed softly. "That's good to hear. Then why do you suppose he packed up and left?"

"How should I know? We've been having a great time this week. We talked about that when we went to get the cocoa, but there was nothing that made me think he was going to leave, especially since he was happy to be here with his uncle. For the last few years, he said, he wasn't able to get back and he really missed Frank."

"Well then, it's a mystery." Mom sipped her coffee. "I guess we'll see him at the wedding. Frank said he agreed to be the best man."

Vera placed her hand over Mom's. "You're going to be so pretty."

"And you'll be my maid of honor, right?"

"Just try and ask someone else." She flashed her mom a huge smile. "There is something I've wanted to talk to you about."

"I'm all ears."

"I lost my job."

"Vera, I am so sorry. It's such a bad time for any company to do that. Did they say why?"

"Right sizing. They think some high school kid can plan and execute a social media plan in conjunction with the marketing team. She was an intern and wormed her way in for half the cost." She shrugged. "Which brings me to my question. Would you mind if I moved home and lived here for a while? I want to start my own social media consulting company. I can live off my savings, but it would go further without having to rent an apartment here until my condo sells. When I came up with the idea, I didn't know about Frank so if you'd rather I didn't, I understand and I'll make it work. But I want to live in Dickens. Permanently."

Mom's grin spread from one side of her face to the other, and even her eyes gleamed. "Is this my Christmas present? Because it is the best gift you could have ever given me."

"That's good. It means I can return your gift to the store and put the cash toward my start-up." She laughed out loud. "You haven't said yes yet."

"Of course you can move home. How fast can you list the condo, and we'll hire a moving company and clean it out right after the first of the year." Mom hopped up to grab a pad and a pen. "We're going to need a to-do list."

"We don't have to get everything done today. After all, it's Christmas Eve and we have to watch *White Christmas* and *The Santa Clause* this afternoon. It's tradition."

"And eat cookies and drink mulled cider," Mom finished.

"Did Frank really need to go to the store, or was that his way of giving us some privacy to talk?"

She bobbed her head from side to side. "A little of both. He needed to pick up the prime rib for dinner tomorrow and the oysters for stew tonight. I did ask him to take his time." She looked at the clock. "Why don't you take Mollie for a walk and when you get back, we'll get everything set up for our mini movie marathon."

Mollie perked up at the sound of her name. She never seemed to miss a trick if it involved a walk or food.

"Come on, girl. Let's stretch our legs before we settle in for the afternoon."

Mollie bounded to the front foyer while Vera set her coffee mug in the sink. She turned and smiled. "Thanks, Mom, for everything."

"That's what mothers are for, to listen to their kids and offer support."

Mollie gave a woof. "You'd better get going before she really starts barking."

"See you in awhile." Feeling lighter than she had just an hour ago, Vera walked into the front hall, put her boots, hat, and coat on, and clipped Mollie's leash on her harness.

Mom poked her head around the corner and said, "Have a good time."

"I have my cell if you need something at the store."

"We're all set. Now go."

Vera closed the door behind her. Her eyes drifted to the driveway, where for some reason, she had hoped to see Tony's old truck. Her heart sank a little.

"Come on, girl."

Mollie trotted down the stairs and headed in the direction of town. She had this route down pat.

10

----

*T*ony watched as Vera and Mollie walked in the direction of the village green. He hadn't gotten very far down the road when he turned around. He hoped he'd get the opportunity to talk to Georgia, and he forgot to leave the ornament he had purchased for Vera.

He dialed the house phone and she picked up on the second ring.

"Hi Georgia, it's Tony."

"This is a nice surprise. Are you okay?"

"I'm fine. Is it possible that you could meet me at the front door?"

"When?"

He could hear the surprise in her voice. "Now? I forgot to leave Vera's Christmas gift and I really want her to have it today."

The front door opened and Georgia stepped onto the porch. He got out of his truck and jogged up the steps, a small box in his hand. The wrapping paper had angels on it.

"Hi." He held out the box. "Can you give this to Vera and ask her to open it right after dinner?"

"Don't you want to give it to her?"

"It's better this way."

Her lips thinned. "Tony, you're making a mistake. You and Vera should talk."

"Merry Christmas, Georgia."

With a heavy heart, he turned and walked back to the truck. This time, he was leaving town, and he'd be back in the city in less than three hours. Where an empty apartment was waiting.

VERA STRETCHED HER ARMS OVERHEAD. She hopped up and glided across the floor in the direction of the kitchen laughing as she did so. "Don't I look just like Rosemary Clooney dancing? All I need is my very own Bing Crosby."

Frank stood up and swept her into his arms. "I'm not Bing, but I'll give you a twirl."

Laughing, he danced her into the kitchen. Mom followed and Vera took the opportunity to change dance partners, putting Mom and Frank together. "I'll fix snacks and we can dive into the next movie."

Mom and Frank danced back into the living room and Vera loaded a tray with finger foods she had made earlier in the day. Who needed a big dinner tonight? She had talked Mom into making the oyster stew for lunch so it was still a part of their traditions.

She carried the tray in and set it on the coffee table, then snapped her fingers and went back in to get napkins. When she came back, a small gift, wrapped in angel paper, was sitting in her spot on the couch.

She held it up. "What's this?"

Mom took Frank's hand. "It's from Tony. He wanted you to open it tonight around dinnertime."

"How did you get this?"

Mom gave her a small smile. "He swung by when you went for your walk."

"Why didn't he stay?"

Frank said, "Open it and let's see what it is."

She eased the paper open and set it aside. "Oh look. It's a wooden box." Her heart skipped in her chest. Why did it feel as if this could change everything?

She took the top off. Nestled in white satin was the wish angel ornament she had seen after they went on the sleigh ride. She picked it up and blinked the tears away.

Mom said, "Vera, that's beautiful."

She swallowed the lump in her throat. "It's a wish angel."

She looked at the doorway. Tony was standing there. A half smile played over his lips.

"Hello."

She hesitated and then flew into his arms. She held him tight and she didn't care that it was excessive as a thank you for her gift.

"You bought me the wish angel."

"I did. I want all your heart wishes to come true." He searched her eyes. "Tell me, how did I do?"

"Fantastic!" She kissed his lips. "Merry Christmas Tony."

He held her close and kissed her. "Merry Christmas, my love."

ONE YEAR LATER...

In the late afternoon, Vera and Tony stood in front of the twenty-foot-tall Christmas tree on the village green in Dickens. The bright lights illuminated the small wedding party.

Vera was dressed in a red wool cape and at the bottom, a gown of white fluttered in the cool breeze. In her hands, she held a small bouquet of white and red roses tied with a deep red velvet ribbon. Tony was handsome in a tailored black tuxedo with a red rose boutonniere pinned to his lapel. He lifted Vera's hand and grazed the back of it with his lips. His eyes were bright and she could see the love in his eyes. Mom and Frank were on either side of them and Pastor Clarissa held a bible in her hands.

Vera took a step closer to Tony. "Did you make your heart wish this year?"

"I made one last year and it's coming true in this very moment." He tenderly kissed her lips. "The only heart wish I made was answered when I met you."

She slid her arm around his neck and kissed him again. "It's Christmas magic."

The End

One year later…

I hope you enjoyed Vera and Tony's story. To meet more residents of Dickens keep reading for a sneak preview of Holly Berries and Hockey Pucks

HOLLY BERRIES AND HOCKEY PUCKS

A DICKENS HOLIDAY ROMANCE

By Lucinda Race

CHAPTER ONE

The door to Jillian Morgan's shop slammed open with a blast of cold October wind. The large white bucket of flowers, which only moments before had been held in her hands, hit the floor. To make matters worse, water sloshed across the floor and soaked her tennis shoes. It wasn't even eight, and this was not the way to start a day. She brushed a wayward curl out of her eyes, and even though she wasn't open yet, she smiled at the potential customer standing in front of her. The only saving grace was that he had remained dry.

"Good morning. How can I help you?"

He pointed to the door over his shoulder. "I just saw your closed sign." The man was close to six feet tall and slender, with short dirty-blond hair and hazel eyes. He gave her a sheepish smile. "I can come back."

"No, it's fine." She didn't remember seeing him in her shop before and wondered if he was just passing through town.

He bent over and retrieved the bucket. "Looks like your day isn't off to a great start." His smile was bright and friendly. "If you get a mop, I'll clean up the water and you can save the flowers."

"No, that's alright, but thank you." She stepped over the puddle to stand behind the counter and brushed back another stray curl. "How can I help you today?"

He looked at the flowers still on the floor and flashed her a grin. "Tell you what. Let me help you clean this up, really, and I'll give you my flower order." He tipped his head to the side. "And for my trouble, you can give me ten percent off."

Since he insisted on being a nice guy, she relented. "I'm Jillian, owner of this shop." She wasn't used to someone offering extraneous help with much of anything, and that included raising her daughter, Melanie. After a moment of hesitation, she said, "Thank you."

He stuck out his hand. "I'm Brett and I've only lived in town for a couple of months."

That kind of explained why she hadn't seen him before. Besides, between running the shop and spending as much time as she could with Melanie, she didn't socialize much. There just weren't enough hours in the day. "Welcome to Dickens. And you're just in time for the holiday season. From Labor Day until the New Year, we're always up to something around here, but mostly it's all about Christmas, considering the name of our little town."

"It's charming. Even though I grew up near Boston, my parents used to bring me to the tree lighting ceremony here every year."

She leaned against the counter. "I think that's one of my favorite nights during the holiday season. It's magical." She could hear the wistful tone in her voice and snapped back to florist mode. "Do you have any idea what you'd like today for an arrangement?"

Brett began to pick up flowers and set them in the now upright five-gallon bucket. "I'm not sure. Something bright and cheery, maybe with some daisies." He held up a lily. "And whatever this is?"

She suppressed a grin. He looked cute with his hands full

of flowers dripping water. "I can include some daisies *and* lilies in the arrangement. Are there any other flowers you'd like?" He continued to fill the bucket with flowers from the floor until the last ones had been scooped up. "Why don't you look around and see if any of the arrangements in the cooler strike you, or I'm happy to put together something new."

She hurried through the archway into the back room, where she grabbed the mop and floor bucket. When she came back into the main shop area, Brett was studying each prearranged bouquet with great interest.

"Did you make all of these this morning?"

She dropped the wet mop into the squeeze part and wrung it out and proceeded to wipe up the last of the puddle. "Actually, last night." She pushed the mop and bucket back into the storage room and when she returned, she asked, "Did you find something?"

He gestured to an arrangement that had white roses, lilies, and colorful Gerber daisies. "I like this one. These are much prettier than the supermarket flowers I've been buying." He winced. "Sorry. I've been meaning to come in sooner."

"I'm glad you're here now." She pulled it from the case and pointed to the cards on the counter. "I can have it delivered by lunchtime. If you want to add a card, help yourself."

"Can I take it with me? I'd like to personally deliver it."

She gave him a smile. "The personal touch is always appreciated." She slipped the vase into a protective wrapper and stapled the top. "Is there anything else I can get you?"

"Would it be possible to have an arrangement made up for me each week for the rest of the year? Similar size, but make them with different color schemes each week, and for the holidays, can you create themed arrangements in seasonal colors? Oh, and do you know where I can get a few wreaths?"

"Sure, I can do all of that. Same day and time each week?"

"Yes, please."

She pulled out her order pad and made notes about the

upcoming orders. She was pleased to have the job. "Right before Thanksgiving, I'll have wreaths for sale and if you'd like, I am accepting preorders now."

He pulled out his wallet to pay for the flowers. "Put me down for two large wreaths and if I could pick up the arrangements every Wednesday around four thirty, that would be good."

How sweet. He must have a weekly dinner with his girlfriend. She wondered if Heather, her best friend and owner of the Library Cat Bookstore, might have some idea about this new hunk in town and who he might be dating. "I can definitely do that." She handed him a business card. "I close at five but if there is any time when you're running late, just give me a call and we can figure something out so you'll still be able to pick them up."

"Thanks. That's really nice of you."

She ran his credit card and handed him the electronic pad to sign. "Thank you for your business." She cringed at how perky her voice was, but a steady customer, not just for the bouquets but wreaths too, was a nice boost for the rest of the year. "One last question. Will you want the flowers in vases each week or will you want to reuse the one you have with today's arrangement?"

He picked up the flowers and glanced at the clear cut glass vase. "This is pretty and multipurpose but for next week, let's have another vase. That way they can be washed in between."

"Perfect."

He gave her a warm smile that made the gold in his eyes sparkle. "Jillian, I'll see you next Wednesday."

With that, he was gone. She leaned against the counter and watched as he disappeared down the street. He was handsome. Not that she needed a complication of the male variety.

Her cell pinged. It was her mom. Her daughter was asking if they were still going to the skating rink tonight. There were signups for hockey and she was determined to make the team.

Without hesitation, she answered, *Yes.* She wanted her daughter to gain the same sense of confidence on the ice she'd had as a kid. Hockey had given her more than just confidence; it had helped pay her way through college, and that's where she had met Melanie's father, even if he had turned out to be an absentee dad. He was chasing the dream of becoming financially successful and maybe someday he'd figure out she was worth more than a monthly check, fancy gifts for special occasions, and an occasional phone call and an even rarer visit. The last time he had seen her was almost four years ago.

Brett carried the vase of flowers to his car. A smile played over his face. Jillian was a surprise; he hadn't expected the owner of Petals to be a pretty young woman who jolted his heart into action. It had been a while since Racine had broken off their engagement and he had no interest in getting involved with anyone new, but it felt good to appreciate the pretty woman with cornflower-blue eyes and blond curls. She was the picture of the girl next door and he was already looking forward to next Wednesday. But first a quick stop at his mom's work, and then he had signed up to start coaching the local youth hockey team and tonight was the first practice.

"Mom, where are you?" He walked through the empty kitchen and carried the vase into the living room, where his mom was sitting in his father's recliner, a box of tissues on her lap and discarded ones littering the floor.

Setting the vase of flowers on the coffee table, he said, "Hey, Mom." His voice was gentle as he dropped to one knee and touched her hand. "What's going on?" His heart was cement in his chest.

Chapter One

Her hazel eyes were rimmed red and bloodshot. "Brett, when did you get here? I must have lost track of time."

"Just now." He pointed to the table. "Surprise."

She patted a hand over her chic-styled silvery-blond hair and placed a freckled hand against his cheek. "Are those for me?"

"They are. I finally made time to investigate the flower shop and I just had to pick some up. Dad always bought you flowers." A fresh wave a grief washed over him as he remembered all the Wednesdays his dad had come home carrying a bright bouquet for her.

"Your father brought me a bouquet every week all the years we were married."

"I remember sometimes he picked wildflowers. I think those were some of your favorites."

Her eyes got a faraway look. "Before we moved to Dickens, we had that huge flower garden where I could cut them every day. Every table in our home had vases of colorful blooms during the summer."

"And Dad bought different flowers every week." He handed her a tissue.

She dried her cheeks. "I'm glad you came over today, and thank you for the flowers. They're lovely, but you should find a special girl you can buy flowers for every week, and not your mother." A sad smile graced her mouth.

"Mom, I don't have time to date. I'm still unpacking my apartment and getting used to my new job." He eased back on the sofa. "But I did make a call to the youth hockey club. At work, someone mentioned they were looking for an assistant coach." He gave a one-shouldered shrug. "I thought it'd be good to get back on the ice."

"Is this a pre-Christmas miracle?" Mom flashed him a genuinely pleased smile. "You haven't held a hockey stick in over ten years."

"I don't want to rehash the past, Mom, but I can still skate,

78

and who knows? Maybe there's a kid that would be interested in learning from me." He got up and grabbed a small trash can. "I'll clean this up, but I do need to get to work. Any chance you'd want to make meatloaf tomorrow night for dinner, with baby carrots and all the good stuff?"

She shook a finger at him. "I know you have an ulterior motive to get me off the chair, but how can I say no to my favorite son asking for his favorite meal, and in the middle of the week?"

"I'm your only kid, so I'd better be your favorite." He dropped a kiss on her cheek. "If you need anything before tomorrow, give me a call."

She stood up and gave him a hard hug. "Be patient with me."

He could hear the catch in her voice. "I will. Everyone says the first year is the hardest. But you've got me and we'll get through all the firsts together." He held her tight, his chin resting on top of her head. "I think we should go out for Thanksgiving dinner. There's plenty of time to make a reservation." He didn't want to tell her he already had. "We'll talk about it tomorrow night."

"I'm not sure, but I'll think about it." She released him with a final squeeze. "Thanks for stopping. I woke up feeling blue and you added a sparkle to my day."

"Why don't you go to the library today, and tomorrow the market? Or better yet, you could stop at that little bookstore in town. You might meet some people."

"Brett, you're pushing me again." She gave him a small poke "You need to get to work and I have a shopping list to make."

"I'll call you later."

"You'll do no such thing; you don't need to hover. Besides, you have hockey practice tonight."

This time, the smile reached her eyes and his internal knot relaxed.

"That's something I haven't said in a long time. Have fun." She opened the kitchen door and ushered him out. "See you at six tomorrow." She closed the door behind him, effectively pushing him along.

His parents had moved to Dickens in January, and his dad had been diagnosed with cancer in March. He'd been with his father in the final weeks of his life and had helped take care of him. It was only after his dad passed that he had found a job and officially moved to Dickens. And now, it had been four months and he was learning to live without his rock. Sadly, there hadn't been time for his mom to make new friends or find a support network before Dad had gotten so sick. Hopefully today would be the first step if she'd go the bookstore or library; one thing she had always loved was to read.

He looked back at the one-story house where his parents had planned to spend their retirement years and his heart ached for what would never be. Life rarely turned out as you planned and Brett knew that firsthand. His dream career and his engagement were both like wisps of smoke, gone with the wind.

FOLLOW ME ON SOCIAL MEDIA

- Like my Facebook page
- Join Lucinda's Heart Racer's Reader Group on Facebook
- Twitter @lucindarace
- Instagram @Lucindaraceauthor
- BookBub
- Goodreads
- Pinterest

LOVE TO READ?

OTHER BOOKS BY LUCINDA RACE:

The Crescent Lake Winery Series 2021
Blends
Breathe
Crush
Blush
Vintage
Bouquet

A Dickens Holiday Romance
Holiday Heart Wishes
Holly Berries and Hockey Pucks

Last Chance Beach
Shamrocks are a Girl's Best Friend Feb 2022

LOVE TO READ CONTINUED...

It's Just Coffee Series 2020
The Matchmaker and The Marine

The MacLellan Sisters Trilogy
Old and New
Borrowed
Blue

The Loudon Series
The Loudon Series Box Set
Between Here and Heaven
Lost and Found
The Journey Home
The Last First Kiss
Ready to Soar
Love in the Looking Glass
Magic in the Rain

Award-winning and best-selling author Lucinda Race is a life-long fan of romantic fiction. As a young girl, she spent hours reading romance novels and getting lost in the hope they represent. While her friends dreamed of becoming doctors and engineers, her dreams were to become a writer—a romance novelist.

As life twisted and turned, she found herself writing nonfiction but longed to turn to her true passion. After developing the storyline for The Loudon Series, it was time to start living her dream. Her fingers practically fly over computer keys as she weaves stories about strong women and the men who love them.

Lucinda lives with her husband and their two little dogs, a miniature long hair dachshund and a shih tzu mix rescue, in the rolling hills of western Massachusetts. When she's not at her day job, she's immersed in her fictional worlds. And if she's not writing romance novels, she's reading everything she can get her hands on. It's too bad her husband doesn't cook, but a very good thing he loves takeout.